A Tale for Easter

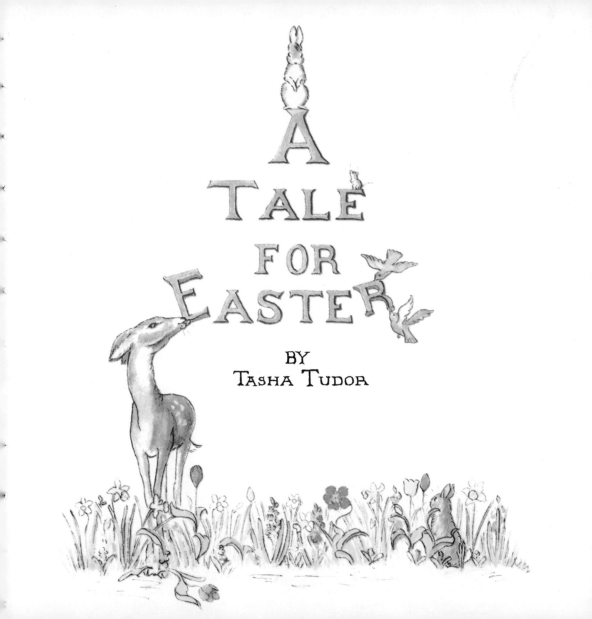

A TALE FOR EASTER

BY
TASHA TUDOR

Library of Congress Cataloging-in-Publication Data:
Tudor, Tasha. A tale for Easter. SUMMARY: You can guess
Easter is coming when you get a new dress, have hot
cross buns, and wake up to colored eggs, baby ducklings,
and a bunny rabbit. {1. Easter–Fiction} I. Title.
PZ7.T8228Tal   1989   {E}   88-30675
ISBN: 0-394-84404-1; 0-394-94404-6 (lib. bdg.)

Manufactured in the United States of America
1 2 3 4 5 6 7 8 9 0

A TALE FOR EASTER

TO
LITTLE
ANN
NEWELL

You can never tell what might happen on Easter.

You're not always sure when it is coming, even though you go to Sunday School.

You can guess it is near

when Mama makes you stand still while she fits a new dress on you.

But it is only when Good Friday comes,

and you have Hot Cross Buns for tea, that you know
for certain Easter will be the day after tomorrow.

On Saturday you go and ask the chickens

to lay you plenty of Easter eggs.

If you have been very good

the whole year through, the night before Easter you
will dream the loveliest dreams.

One will be about a wee fawn,

who makes you as light as thistledown and takes you on her back and gallops through the woods and fields.

She shows you rabbits

smoothing their sleek coats for Easter morning.

And mice with beady eyes

and shining whiskers.

Little lambs, too,

in fields of buttercups.

And Easter ducklings

swimming among the lily pads.

If you have been especially good

and done nearly everything you have been told, she
will take you up, up, over the misty moisty clouds,
where the bluebirds dye their feathers, and the
robins find the colour for their eggs.

But this is only if you have been good

and can find the star dust on daffodils with your eyes tight shut.

And when you wake up in the morning

there isn't any fawn at all, and you are just you again. But often there are coloured eggs in your shoes or in your best bonnet.

Or a basket of ducklings

beside your bowl of porridge.

There might even be a bunny in Grandma's
                                    rocking chair.

You can never really tell, for anything might happen on Easter.